Christmas Music
For Guitar Ensemble
Score and 1st Guitar
MB98302

W9-DEV-879

Free Guitar 2, 3 and 4 parts available online!
Visit: www.melbay.com/98302

BILL'S MUSIC SHELF

Contents

Score

Contents

Guitar I

Introduction

To Noel Elizabeth Miller

This volume presents fome of the most beloved repertoire for the Christmas season. Some works are well known, others will sound fresh and new to most players. These piees are intended for multiple guitars for both classroom use and performance at concerts. It is desirable to use several guitars on each part. A good idea is to rotate players on different parts to increase their reading abililty on both lower and upper strings.

All arrangements are provided with a keyboard part in the conductor's score. The keyboard part will not always duplicate hte guitar parts above. This part is optional and may be used for support in rehearsal or in concert, or both. '

A special word of gratitude to Peter Ciarelli for the beautiful work he did in preparing the manuscripts on Finale software for publication. And a final word of thanks to my wife and family for their patience dureing the publication process.

Sincerely,

Don Miller

Score

A Virgin Unspotted

(for finger-style or flat-pick guitar)

William Billings
1746-1800
Arr. Don Miller

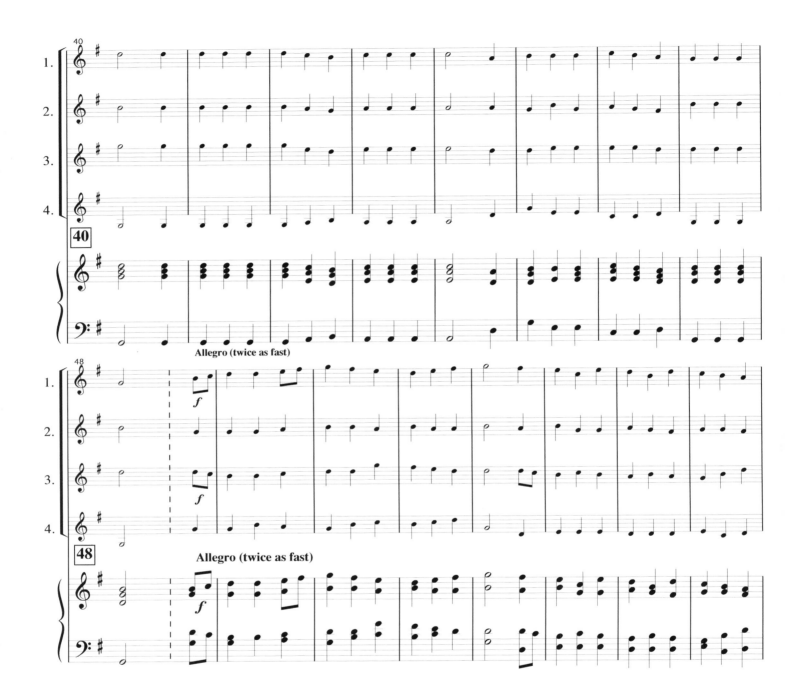

Angels We Have Heard On High

W.A. Mozart- Alleluia; Ave Verum Corpus
(for finger-style or flat-pick guitar)

Traditional
Arr. Don Miller

As Lately We Watched

(for finger-style or flat-pick guitar)

Austrian Folk Song

Arr. Don Miller

15

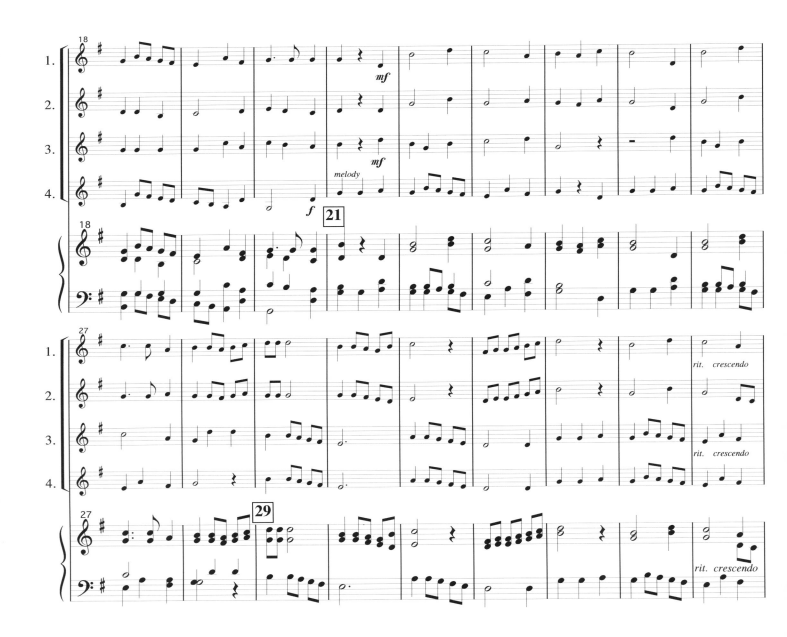

Carol of the Bells

(for finger-style or flat-pick guitar)

Mikola Leontovich

Arr. Don Miller

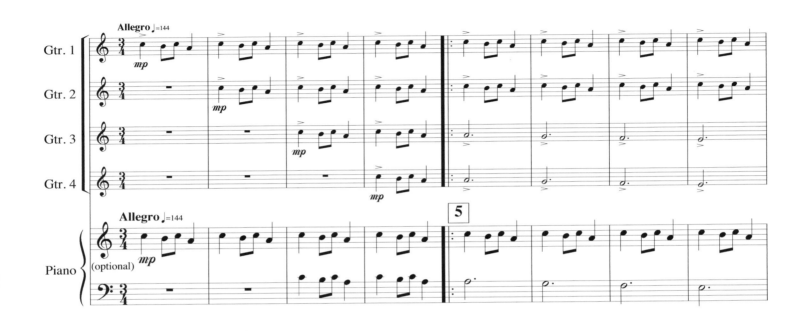

Christmas Morn Is Dawning

(for finger-style or flat-pick guitar)

German Folksong

Arr. Don Miller

Ding Dong Merrily On High

(for finger-style or flat-pick guitar)

French Melody

Arr. Don Miller

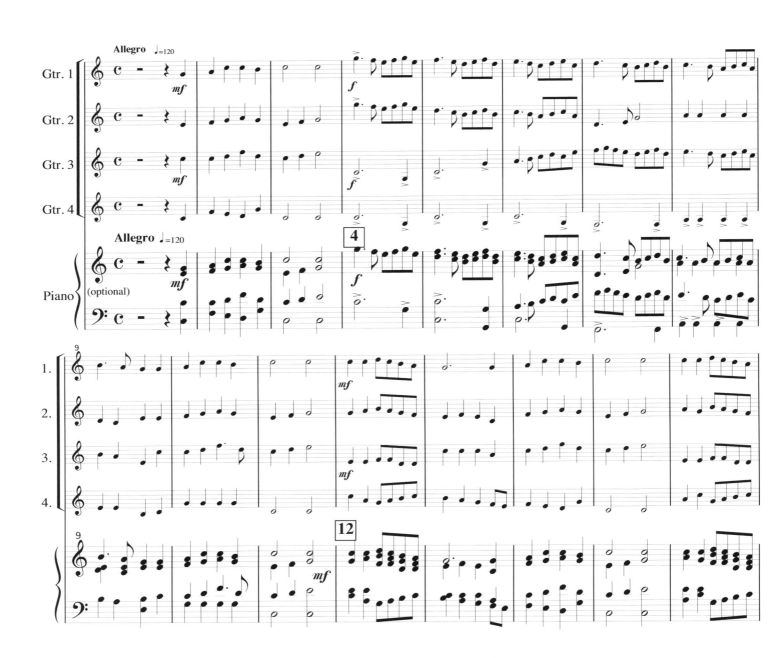

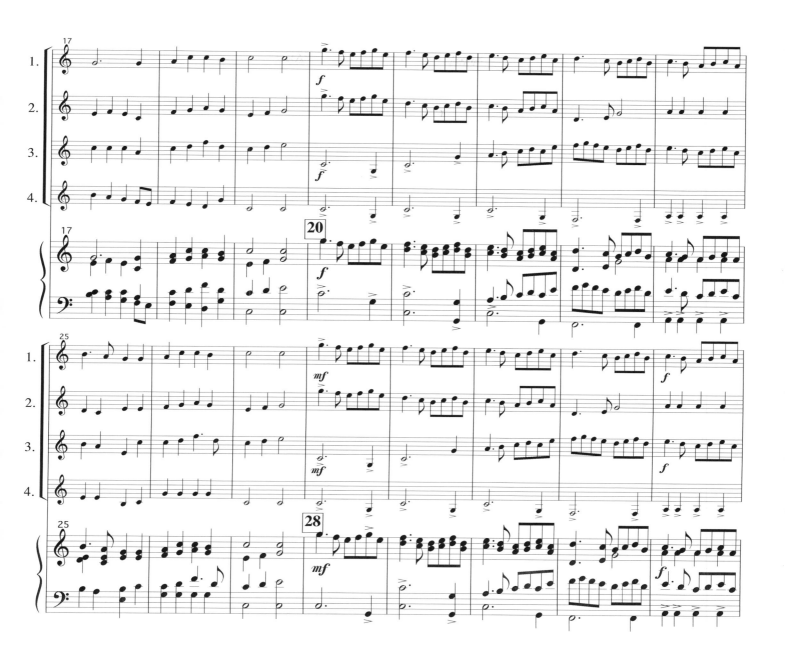

El Noi De Le Mare?

What Shall We Give?

(for finger-style or flat-pick guitar)

Catalonian Carol

Arr. Don Miller

Noel Nouvelet

A Little New Noel

(for finger-style or flat-pick guitar)

French Carol

Arr. Don Miller

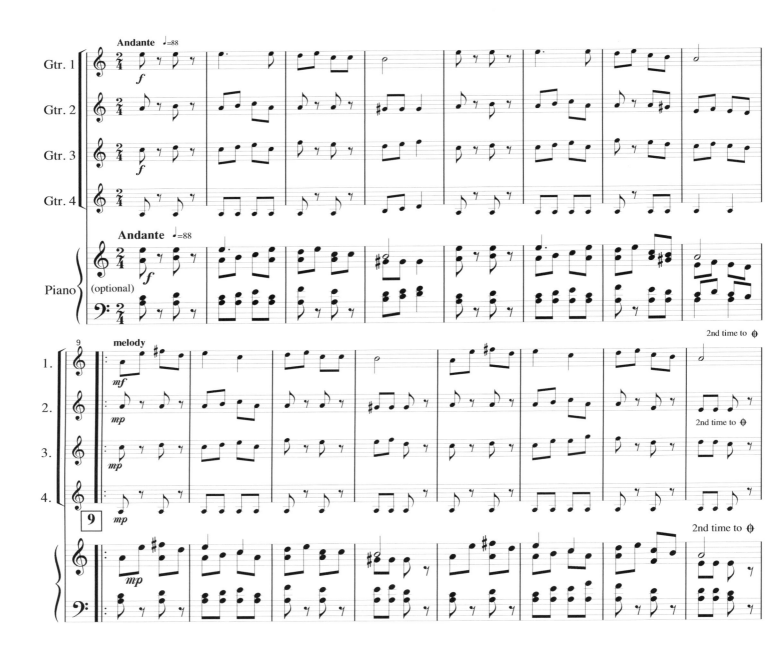

O, Dearest Love

Paraphrase: Lo, How A Rose E'r Blooming

(for finger-style or flat-pick guitar)

Hans Leo Hassler

(1564-1612)

Arr. Don Miller

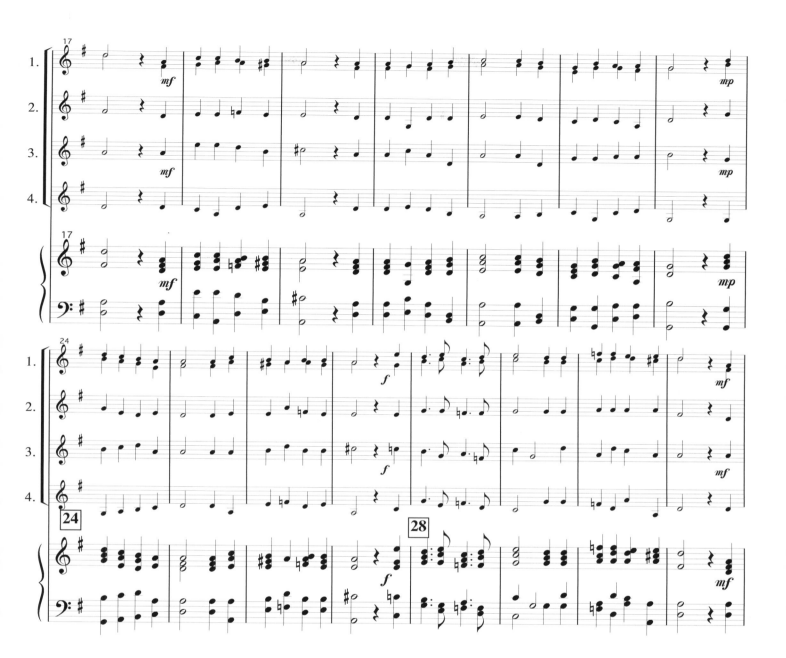

Pat-A-Pan

(for finger-style or flat-pick guitar)

French Carol

Arr. Don Miller

Guitar I

A Virgin Unspotted

(for finger-style or flat-pick guitar)

William Billings
1746-1800
Arr. Don Miller

Gtr. 1

Rit. on repeat

Angels We Have Heard On High

W.A. Mozart- <u>Alleluia</u>; <u>Ave Verum Corpus</u>

(for finger-style or flat-pick guitar)

Traditional
Arr. Don Miller

Gtr. 1

As Lately We Watched

(for finger-style or flat-pick guitar)

Austrian Folk Song
Arr. Don Miller

Gtr. 1

Carol of the Bells

(for finger-style or flat-pick guitar)

Mikola Leontovich
Arr. Don Miller

Gtr. 1

Christmas Morn Is Dawning

(for finger-style or flat-pick guitar)

German Folksong
Arr. Don Miller

Gtr. 1

Ding Dong Merrily On High

(for finger-style or flat-pick guitar)

French Melody
Arr. Don Miller

Gtr. 1

El Noi De Le Mare?

What Shall We Give?

(for finger-style or flat-pick guitar)

Catalonian Carol
Arr. Don Miller

Gtr. 1

Noel Nouvelet
A Little New Noel
(for finger-style or flat-pick guitar)

French Carol
Arr. Don Miller

Gtr. 1

O, Dearest Love

Paraphrase: Lo, How A Rose E'r Blooming

(for finger-style or flat-pick guitar)

Hans Leo Hassler
(1564-1612)
Arr. Don Miller

Gtr. 1

Divide between two or more players or one player

Decrescendo and ritard

Pat-A-Pan

(for finger-style or flat-pick guitar)

French Carol
Arr. Don Miller

Gtr. 1

EXCELLENCE IN MUSIC!

17289101R00033

Made in the USA
Middletown, DE
16 January 2015